Rex's Specs

Hardback edition published in 2012 by Wayland
Paperback edition published in 2013 by Wayland
Text and illustrations © Jack Hughes 2012

Wayland
338 Euston Road
London NW1 3BH

Wayland Australia
Level 17/207 Kent Street
Sydney, NSW 2000

Commissioning Editor: Victoria Brooker
Design: Lisa Peacock and Steve Prosser

British Library Cataloguing in Publication Data
Hughes, Jack.
Rex's specs. -- (The dinosaur friends)
1. Dinosaurs--Pictorial works--Juvenile fiction.
2. Myopia--Pictorial works--Juvenile fiction.
3. Children's stories--Pictorial works.
I. Title II. Series
823.9'2-dc23

HB ISBN 978 0 7502 7057 1
PB ISBN 978 0 7502 7819 5

Printed in China

Wayland is a division of Hachette Children's Books,
an Hachette UK Company
www.hachette.co.uk

Rex's Specs

Written and illustrated by Jack Hughes

WAYLAND

Rex wore bright red specs. Rex's specs were fantastic.

With his specs Rex could see a really long way.

Rex could see for miles.

He would climb to the top of the big hill with Steggie, Dachy and Emmy, and amaze them with stories of the distant lands they could see.

However, without his specs, Rex could see very little at all.

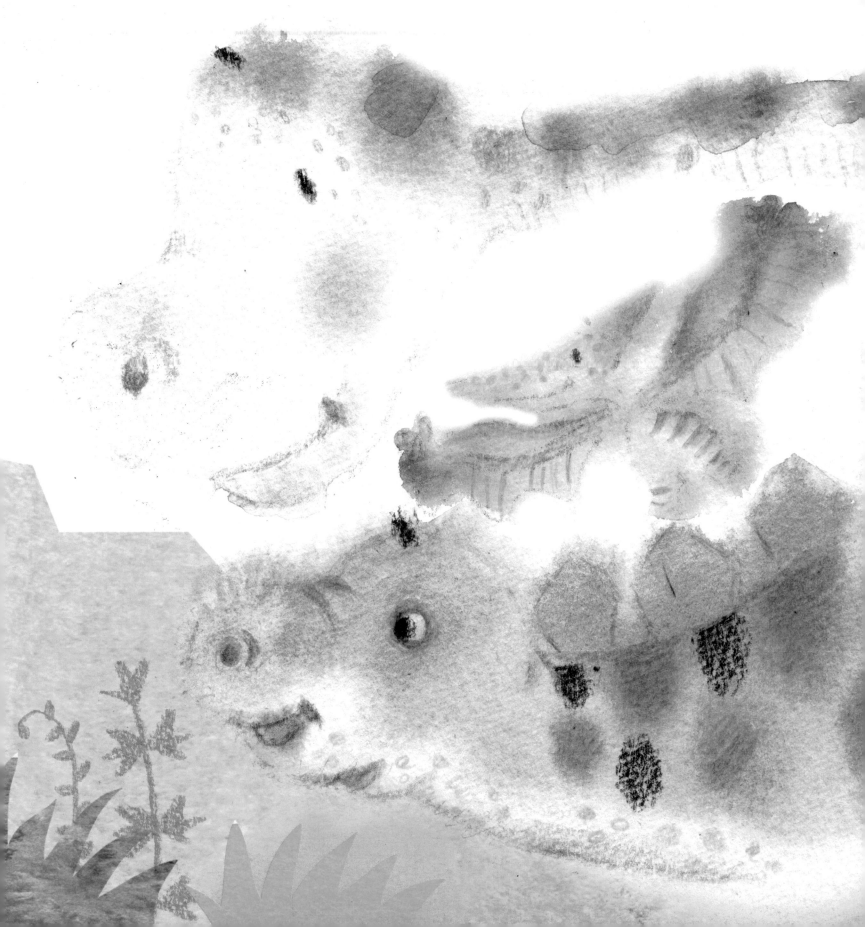

Rex didn't like wearing his specs.

He wished he could be like everyone else.

Rex thought his friends didn't like his specs.

But, secretly, they all wanted specs like Rex.

One day, Rex decided to go out to play without his specs. He wandered off towards the forest in search of his friends. "Hi, Emmy," said Rex.

But it wasn't Emmy. It was a SNAKE!!!! Ssssss...
"Aargh!" cried Rex, when he heard the snake's
hiss, and he ran away as fast as he could.

Rex kept running until he came across a cave. He could see someone hiding in there. He was sure it was his friend, Steggie. "Steggie, is that you?" Rex called. "Are you playing hide and seek with Emmy? Can I play?"

But it wasn't Steggie. It was a BEAR!!!! GRRRRR...

GRRRRR!!!

'Aargh,' shrieked Rex. "You're not Steggie!"
And he turned and fled.

Rex ran and ran until he was far away from the bear's cave. Feeling tired and upset, he flopped down by the lake for a rest. "Where are my friends?" he cried.

But Rex hadn't seen the crocodile in the lake.
The crocodile who had just spotted his
afternoon snack...

SNAP!
SNAP!

"Eek! CROCODILE!!!!" yelled Rex, jumping to his feet
and scrabbling out of reach of the crocodile's mouth
just before its jaws snapped shut.

Rex kept running until **BANG!!** He hit a big tree.

But it wasn't a tree. It was Rex's friend, Emmy.

"Hello there, Rex. Are you OK?" she said.
"We've all been looking for you!"

Steggie and Dachy arrived.
"You forgot your specs, Rex.
Your mum was worried."

"I didn't forget them," Rex said, sadly. "I just decided
not to wear them anymore. I don't like them!"

"But Rex, we all LOVE your specs!"
his friends shouted out excitedly.
"We wish WE had specs just like yours!"
"You do?" asked Rex.
"YES!" they replied.

Rex put on his specs and beamed from ear to ear.
He could see his friends clearly again.

"Come on, Rex!" they called. "Let's go to the very top of Big Hill and look out over the valley. Then you can tell us all about your adventure today."